Jennie and the Black Stockings

by Jane Belk Moncure
illustrated by
Lydia Halverson

Published by The Dandelion House
A Division of The Child's World

for distribution by **VICTOR** **BOOKS** a division of SP Publications, Inc.

WHEATON. ILLINOIS 60187

Offices also in
Whitby, Ontario, Canada
Amersham-on-the-Hill, Bucks, England

*This book is dedicated to my mother,
Jennie Wannamaker Belk, to whom the
events in this story really happened.*

Jane Belk Moncure

Published by The Dandelion House, A Division of The Child's World, Inc.
© 1984 SP Publications, Inc. All rights reserved. Printed in U.S.A.

A Book for Early Readers.

Library of Congress Cataloging in Publication Data

Moncure, Jane Belk.
  Jennie and the black stockings.

  Summary: Little Jennie is responsible for her father's
loss of a year's supply of cotton, but that good man
teaches her that God gets us through hard times.
  [1. Christian life-Fiction]   I. Halverson,
Lydia, ill.   II. Title.
PZ7.M739Je   1984   [E]   84-7036
ISBN 0-89693-225-7

1 2 3 4 5 6 7 8 9 10 11 12 R 90 89 88 87 86 85 84

2

Jennie and the Black Stockings

Jennie climbed the ladder to the hayloft. She
wanted to watch the men unload the wagons
full of cotton bales.

"Best year we've ever had," said Papa. "The Lord has blessed us."

"Yep, best cotton crop I've ever seen," said Mark, the hired man.

Then Papa saw Jennie.

"There's the best tomboy on the farm! Be careful, daughter," he called.

"Yes, Papa." Jennie waved.

Soon the cotton bales were stacked like a giant playhouse in the back yard.

Jennie took her little brother, Frank, to see the wonderful, cotton-bale house.

They peeked inside.

"Come on, Frank. Let's play house," said Jennie.

She crawled through a little opening be-tween the cotton bales. Frank followed.

Jennie looked around. It was just like a cozy house.

"Now, I'll be the mother and you be the child," said Jennie.

"I'm hungry," said Frank.

"I'll fix soup," said Jennie, pretending. She gathered up bits of dry cotton.

Just then Mark came by.

"Hush," whispered Jennie. "Don't let Mark hear us. We're hiding."

Mark did not see the children. He threw his jacket over one of the cotton bales and walked away. Something fell out of the pocket.

Jennie picked it up. It was a box of matches.
Papa had warned Jennie never to play with
matches. But in her excitement, Jennie forgot.

"I'll cook your soup now, Frank," she said, striking a match.

Puff! The dry cotton flamed . . . burned! In a second the fire got bigger . . . and very hot!

Jennie grabbed little Frank and pulled him outside. Black smoke swirled around them.

"Fire!" she screamed.

"Mama! Papa! Fire! Help!"

Papa and Mark came running from the field.

"Fire! Fire!" they called.

Papa rang the big farm bell.

"Fire! Fire!" he yelled.

Mama and Mark ran to the well to get water.

"Fire! Help!"

Neighbors saw the smoke and came running!
They formed a line from the well to the fire,

pouring water on the flames as fast as they
could.

Then, down the road came the horse-drawn
fire wagon from town.

Cheers went up! But by now many bales
were smoking.

Terrified, Jennie stood on the porch steps, clutching little Frank.

"Oh, what will Papa say? What will he do to me?" Jennie asked. She knew she had done a terrible thing. She hid her face in her hands and cried. Little Frank cried too.

When the fire was out, Jennie ran to Papa.
She was sure Papa would punish her.

"Oh, Papa," she sobbed. "I . . . I didn't
mean to strike the match. Oh, I'm sorry. Oh
Papa, I'm so sorry."

Papa lifted her into his arms. "We're all sorry, Jennie," he said. "We've lost a year's supply of cotton."

Jennie sobbed. "Oh, Papa, it was my fault."

"There, there, Jennie. Don't cry."

"But the cotton . . ." Jennie cried. "What will we do without cotton?"

"We can grow more cotton. But you children . . . are all we have. And you're safe. Thank God. And we'll trust Him to see us through this somehow," Papa said.

After awhile, the men loaded the black cotton onto the wagons.

Still crying, Jennie asked, "Papa, what will you do with the cotton? Will you throw it away?"

Papa held her close. "We won't have to throw it all away. There's some good cotton

left. There's not enough to ship to Richmond.
But we can sell it to the stocking factory. They
make black stockings. All the ladies in town
wear black stockings. Why, you can even hang
up a black stocking for Christmas. God will
help us get by, Jennie. Now, don't cry any-
more.''

Sure enough, on Christmas Eve, Jennie hung up a black stocking. Still, she felt sad about what she had done. She knew Papa had lost much of his cotton crop. There wasn't much money for gifts.

Jennie crawled into Papa's lap. "Will we have Christmas in the morning?" she asked.

"Of course we will have Christmas," he said. "We may not have lots of presents, but we will have Christmas. Jennie, you know we trust in God to get us through the hard times as well as the good times. God loves us, Jennie."

On Christmas morning, Jennie took down
her stocking. It was stuffed with oranges, nuts,
and peppermint sticks. A little rag doll was
peeking out of the top.

And way down in the toe of the stocking was
a letter from Papa. You can read what it said.

December 25, 1905

Dear Jennie,

Christmas is a birthday party! Did you know that? Christmas is Jesus' birthday. And the real reason we have Christmas is to celebrate it!

God loves us and gives us gifts all year. God's gifts are not wrapped in boxes, but they are everywhere in His world. Gifts like the feather-soft snowflakes of winter. The pink-purple blossoms of spring. The yellow fields of summer. The brightly-colored leaves of fall.

page 2

But God's greatest gift of love is Jesus, His Son.

Jennie, we can always be sure of God's love. His love never breaks, never burns up like cotton! God's love is seen in the love of your father and mother, your brothers and sisters. It is seen most of all in Jesus.

Remember, Jennie, you can always trust God. He loves you!

Merry Christmas!

Papa

Jennie remembered. When she grew up, she told this story to her children, her grandchildren, and her great grandchildren so that they too would remember to trust God—in the good times and the bad.